Panda's New Toy

For Stephen Fry
J.D.

For Nat, who likes toys
H.C.

First published 1999 by Walker Books Ltd
87 Vauxhall Walk, London SE11 5HJ

10 9 8 7 6 5 4 3 2 1

Text © 1999 Joyce Dunbar
Illustrations © 1999 Helen Craig

The right of Joyce Dunbar and Helen Craig to be identified
as author and illustrator respectively of this work has been
asserted by them in accordance with the Copyright,
Designs and Patents Act 1988.

This book has been typeset in AT Arta Medium

Printed in Hong Kong

British Library Cataloguing in Publication Data
A catalogue record for this book is
available from the British Library.

ISBN 0-7445-4821-7

Panda's
New Toy

Joyce Dunbar

illustrated by
Helen Craig

WALKER BOOKS
AND SUBSIDIARIES
LONDON • BOSTON • SYDNEY

Panda had a new toy.

It was a cup and a ball.

The ball was fastened

to the cup with

a piece of string.

"How do you play with it?"

asked Gander.

"The game is to swing the ball and
catch it in the cup," said Panda.

"I'll show you."

Panda swung the ball and ...

missed.

He swung it again and ...

missed again!

He swung it and missed,

again ...

and again.

"Can I have a go?" asked Gander.

"Wait until I've got it right,"

said Panda.

Panda swung the ball again ...

and caught it!

"See, Gander. I caught the ball in the cup. That's what you have to do."

"Just watch."

Panda swung the ball ...

and missed!

But then he swung it and

caught it,

again ...

and again.

"Can I have a go now?" asked Gander.

"It might be too difficult for you," said Panda.

"It looks easy," said Gander.

"It's easy for me," said Panda.

"So easy I think I could catch it with my eyes closed. Let's see."

Panda swung the ball and caught
it with his eyes closed.

"Is it my turn now?" asked Gander.
"I think I could even catch it
standing on one leg," said Panda.
"Watch this."

So Panda swung the ball and
caught it standing on one leg.
"That's clever,"
said Gander.

"Is it my turn now?"
"I want to see if I can eat a biscuit
with one paw and catch the ball
with the other," said Panda.

Panda ate a biscuit with one paw
and caught the ball with the other.

"Now it's my turn," said Gander.

"First I want to see if I can swing
on the swing and still catch the ball
in the cup," said Panda.

So Gander pushed
Panda on the
swing ...

while Panda caught the
ball in the cup.
"I think I could be an acrobat,"
said Panda.

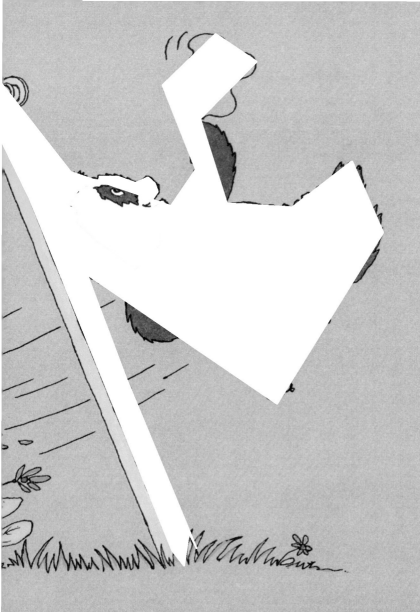

"I think you could," said Gander,

"but it's my turn now."

"I'll just have one last turn,"

  said Panda.

"You've had lots of last turns,"

said Gander.

"A really last turn," said Panda.

So Panda had a really last turn.

But he swung the ball too hard and

broke the string!

Away rolled the ball,

Gander went running to fetch it.

"Now I won't be able to have
a turn," said Gander.
"Yes, you will," said Panda.
And he tied a knot in the string
so that the ball was fastened to
the cup again.

"Good," said Gander.

"Now can I have a go?"

"Let me see if it works first,"
  said Panda. "The string might be
  too long or too short."

"Panda," said Gander.

"What is it?" said Panda.

"I don't care if the string is too
  long or too short.

I don't want to play with that toy
any more. I'm going to play with
the jolly trolley."
"Gander," said Panda.

"What is it?" said Gander.
"It's your turn with the cup and
the ball. *I* want to play with
the jolly trolley."

"Good," said Gander to Panda, "because it's my turn for a ride on the jolly trolley and your turn to pull it along."

And riding along on the
jolly trolley, Gander swung the
ball in the cup and –
caught it!